The Big Block of Chocolate

by Janet Slater Redhead
Illustrated by Christine Dale

READ BY READING Series

Ashton Scholastic
Auckland   Sydney   New York   London   Toronto

Miss Jenny bought some chocolate,
a great big block of chocolate.
She said, "This block of chocolate
is mine and ALL for me."

"Just the very sight of it
brings back the taste delight of it.
I'll savour every bite of it —
but later,
secretly."

Her big dog found the chocolate,
the great big block of chocolate.
He said, "This block of chocolate
is mine and ALL for me."

"Just the very sight of it
brings back the taste delight of it.
I'll savour every bite of it —
but later,
secretly."

Her fat cat found the chocolate,
the great big block of chocolate.
He said, "This block of chocolate
is mine and ALL for me."

"Just the very sight of it
brings back the taste delight of it.
I'll savour every bite of it —
but later,
secretly."

A magpie found the chocolate,
the great big block of chocolate.
She said, "This block of chocolate
is mine and ALL for me."

"Just the very sight of it
brings back the taste delight of it.
I'll savour every bite of it —
but later,
secretly."

The hot sun found the chocolate,
the great big block of chocolate.

It shone down on the chocolate which trickled down the tree.

One small ant found the chocolate,
the great big *stream* of chocolate.

He sang out, *"Brothers! Chocolate!*
Come and share with me."

"Just the very sight of it
brings back the taste delight of it.
We'll savour every bite of it —

but right now,
gleefully."

15

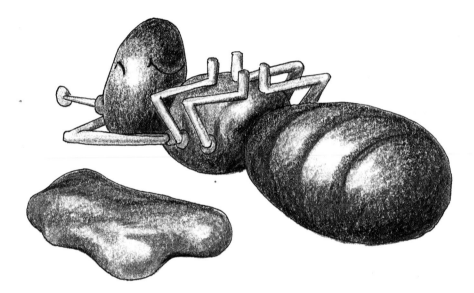